GW01604968
BOX
-O-
JUICE
Fragile
BOX
-O-
SUGAR
YUM
ART
DONUTS

BOX
-O-
JUICE
CRAYONS
Fragile
BOX
-O-
SUGAR
ART
YUM
DONUTS

The Boy Who Loved Boxes

By Michael Albanese Art by Todd Wilkerson

ISBN: 978-1-7328987-3-8

First published by The Weight of Ink in 2022
Written by: Michael Albanese
Illustrated by: Todd Wilkerson

Created in The Town at Trilith, Fayetteville, Georgia
Printed in the United States of America

Please visit TheWeightofInk.com

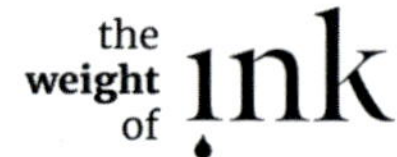

There once was a Boy who loved boxes.

The Boy loved them because he had so much stuff!

He had a box for everything:

Art supplies.

Books. **Building blocks.**

Stuffed animals.

Trains.

The boxes gave his room a sense of order.

And this made The Boy feel happy.

Day by day, The Boy grew up and became a man.

As he got older and the stuff in his life got more complicated,

The Man found bigger and better boxes.

The Man loved them because he had so much stuff!

He had a box for everything:

Emotions.

Faith.

Relationships.

Money.

Work.

The boxes gave him a sense of control.

Then one day…

…something happened in the world.

And his boxes fell apart.

So, he emptied out all the boxes.

Some stuff was missing. Many things were broken.

The Man did not love the boxes anymore.

And this made The Man feel hopeless.

He got on the floor like he did when he played as a boy.

And he sat in the mess.

Maybe he did not need so many boxes.

Maybe he just needed one box—
the right box, he thought.

He could buy a fancier box.

He was wealthy enough to do that.

When that box did not work, The Man thought he could build a more durable box.

He was smart enough to do that.

But that box did not work either.

Over time, The Man realized he just could not do it himself.

Maybe this box could not be found with his eyes or made with his hands.

Then one day…

…something happened in his heart.

A large box appeared.

This one was different than all the other boxes The Man had ever known.

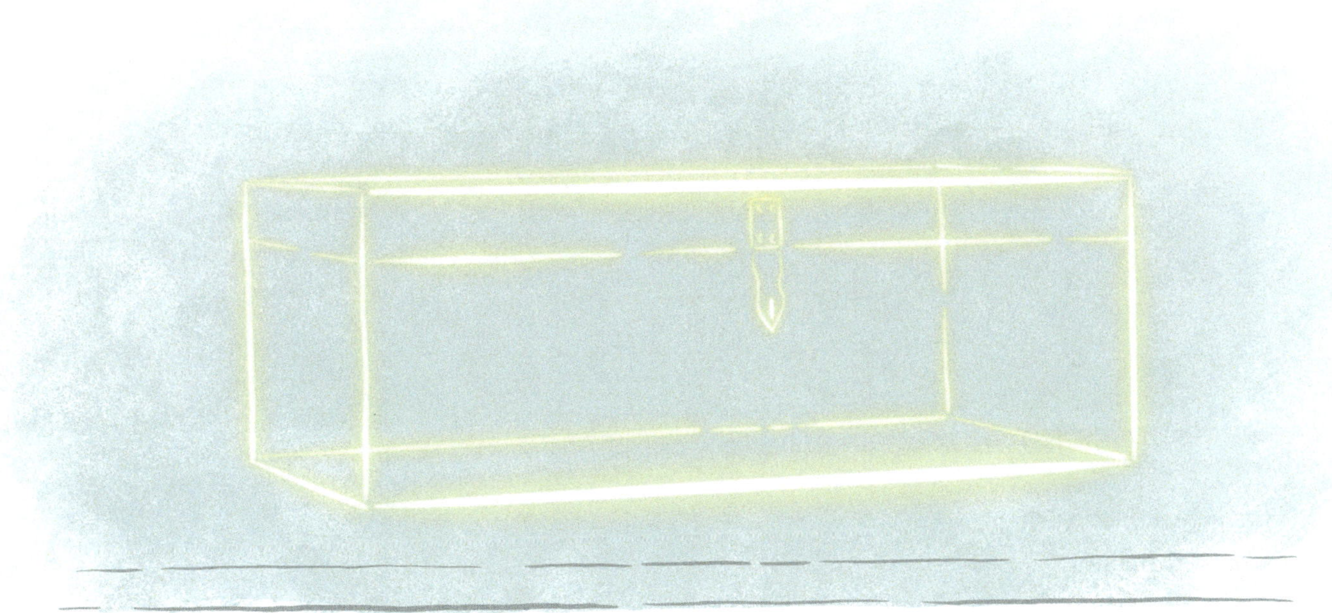

So, he began to fill it with all of his things.

Even the broken parts.

DREAM
Journal
BANK

The Man loved this box because he could finally see all of his stuff!

This box gave him a sense of purpose.

And this made The Man feel something he had never felt before…

… peace.

MICHAEL ALBANESE is a writer, entrepreneur and coffee aficionado. After many years adventuring in New York City and Los Angeles, he relocated to his home state of Georgia. Michael lives and dreams with his wife, actress Wynn Everett, and their two daughters in South Atlanta. This is his third children's book.

TODD WILKERSON is an actor, freelance illustrator and ice cream aficionado. He is a New Yorker who has lived in Los Angeles for the past twelve years with his wife, two daughters and a dog that enjoys watching him draw. This is his first picture book.

BILLS
MA
THANK YOU
THIS
SIDE
UP

Made in the USA
Monee, IL
04 March 2022